THE WORLD OF
ASTRID LINDGREN

Happy Times in
Noisy Village

OXFORD
UNIVERSITY PRESS

Great Clarendon Street, Oxford OX2 6DP
Oxford University Press is a department of the University of Oxford.
It furthers the University's objective of excellence in research, scholarship,
and education by publishing worldwide. Oxford is a registered trade mark of
Oxford University Press in the UK and in certain other countries

ASTRID LINDGREN COMPANY

Translated from the Swedish by Susan Beard
English translation © Susan Beard 2015

The Children
of Noisy Village

This translation of *Happy Times in Noisy Village* originally published in Swedish
published by arrangement with The Astrid Lindgren Company

The moral rights of the author, illustrator, and translator have been asserted

First published in 1949 as *Mera om oss barn i Bullerbyn* by Rabén & Sjögren, Sweden
All foreign rights are handled by The Astrid Lindgren Company, Stockholm, Sweden
For more information, please contact info@astridlindgren.se

First published in English by Oxford University Press 2015
First published in this edition 2021 by Oxford University Press

Database right Oxford University Press (maker)

British Library Cataloguing in Publication Data

Data available

ISBN: 978-0-19-277625-9

3 5 7 9 10 8 6 4 2

Printed and bound by CPI Group (UK) Ltd, Croydon, CR0 4YY

Paper used in the production of this book is a natural,
recyclable product made from wood grown in sustainable forests.
The manufacturing process conforms to the environmental
regulations of the country of origin.

Happy Times in Noisy Village

BY **ASTRID LINDGREN**

ILLUSTRATED BY **MINI GREY**

TRANSLATED BY **SUSAN BEARD**

OXFORD
UNIVERSITY PRESS

THE WORLD OF
ASTRID LINDGREN

BOOKS BY ASTRID LINDGREN
ILLUSTRATED BY MINI GREY

CONTENTS

All of us Noisy Village Children

This is Lasse, Bosse and me, and Olle and Britta and Anna. We are the children who live in Noisy Village. I live at Middle Farm with Lasse and Bosse, Olle lives at South Farm, and Britta and Anna live at North Farm.

Grandad lives at North Farm too. He would live there, of course, seeing as he is Britta and Anna's grandad. But all of us here in Noisy Village call him Grandad because he is the only grandad we have.

As for mums and dads, we have a quite a lot of those. I mean, there is a mum and dad at North

1

Farm, and a mum and dad at Middle Farm, and a mum and dad at South Farm. After that there is no one else at all here in Noisy Village. Apart from Agda, who helps Mum, and Oskar who is our farmhand, and Kalle who is the farmhand at North Farm. Oh yes, at South Farm there is one more person. A tiny, tiny person. She is Olle's little sister Kerstin, who he got a few months ago. But when you are so small that you can't talk and can't walk, you're not really a proper

person at all, are you? Although Olle thinks his sister is more important than the king himself.

Now I've told you about everyone who lives in Noisy Village. Except I haven't told you about Svipp, who is Olle's dog, and Malkolm and Milo and Sessan, our cats, and Albertina, Bosse's hen, and all our cows and horses and sheep and pigs and rabbits. But they are not people, of course. Although Svipp is almost as clever as a human being and cleverer than a girl, says Lasse.

We Go Sledging

Noisy Village is very high up, and when we walk to Storby Village, where we go to school and where the shop is, it's downhill almost all the way. But when we walk home again we have to go uphill, of course. Lasse says that when he grows up and becomes a cog-spinning-sprocket-swashing engineer he will invent a hill that tilts up and down like a seesaw, so that you are always going downhill.

Those hills from Noisy Village down to Storby Village are the best sledging slopes you can possibly imagine. We spend all the Christmas holidays sledging there.

The day after Boxing Day this year, when we

had read all the books we had for Christmas, and eaten up all our ginger biscuits, Lasse got out the big sledge we use to carry logs. And we set off down the slopes, all of us Noisy Village children. Lasse was steering.

'Look out below!' we all shouted, as loudly as we could. That wasn't really necessary, because there is hardly ever anyone on our slopes. But it was fun to shout anyway, as we came swooshing down at top speed. Then it was quite difficult trudging up to Noisy Village again, and Lasse talked a lot about that hill he was going to invent, the one that tilted up and down.

'Can't you invent it straight away?' asked Bosse.

But Lasse said that a hill like that would need so much dynamite and so many pulleys and nuts and bolts, that it would take ten years to make. And we couldn't wait that long.

When at last we had dragged the sledge up all the hills and were just about to sit on it again outside our barn, Dad and Olle's dad and Britta and Anna's dad came out through the barn door. And Dad said:

'Hey kids, can we borrow the sledge for a while?'

And then he sat on the sledge, and so did Uncle Erik and Uncle Nils as well. And off they went down the slopes. We waited. But when they came back they wanted to borrow the sledge again, because it was such fun riding on it. Honestly, to think that grown-ups can be so childish!

So then we fetched North Farm's log sledge and rode down after the dads. When we were halfway down the first slope we saw them lying in a snow drift, laughing their heads off.

'Call that steering, Erik?' said Dad.

It was completely impossible to get them to give the sledge back. They rode on it over and over and over again, until Britta and Anna's mum came and told Uncle Erik that he had to go home and chop some wood.

'We're never allowed to have any fun,' said Uncle Erik, laughing and brushing off all the snow.

When we were on our own again we had a race. Britta and Anna and I had North Farm's sledge, and Lasse and Bosse and Olle had Middle Farm's sledge. We pretended they were Viking ships sailing on the ocean. Lasse called the boys'

sledge Long Snake and
we called ours Sweet Briar
Rose, even though Lasse said it
was an idiotic name for a Viking ship.

'That doesn't matter as long as it's beautiful,' we said, because once we had named our ship we didn't want to change it just because Lasse thought it was idiotic.

The race was so exciting. Long Snake and Sweet Briar Rose were exactly side by side all the time. And all the time the boys yelled:

'Look at little Sweet Briar Rose, Watch out now 'cos over she goes!'

But I have to tell you that it was Long Snake that tipped over, not us. It ran right into a snowdrift. Sweet Briar Rose sailed on beautifully all the way down to the tall pine tree at the foot of the second hill, where the goal was.

'That's what
happens when
people show off,'
said Britta to Lasse.

But Lasse had banged
his head on the root of a tree
and had a big bump on his forehead,
so we gave up sledging. Anyway, it
had become very dark and we were very
hungry. So we went home.

We Stay Up
and Welcome in
the New Year

On New Year's Eve morning, as I was sitting in the kitchen eating porridge, Britta and Anna came in looking very excited. And Britta said:

'Lisa, do you want to welcome in the New Year with us?'

'Oh yes, I'd really like to do that,' I said, because I thought it was a good idea. But first I had to ask Mum if I was allowed to stay up until 12 at night when the New Year comes. And I was allowed. We decided straight away that we would welcome in the New Year in my room. Mum said we could have apples and nuts and juniper berry cordial for our party.

Lasse and Bosse came in immediately afterwards and I said:

'Britta and I are going to welcome in the New Year tonight!'

And then Lasse said:

'Bosse and Olle and I are going to do that too. We decided it ages ago.'

But I'm very sure they made that up on the spot, and that the boys were going to welcome in the New Year just because we were.

We ran off to Grandad and asked him if he would like to welcome in the New Year with us. But Grandad said he was always so sleepy in the evenings. Grandad is *ever* so kind! He went to his wardrobe and brought out lots of small lumps of lead and gave them to us.

'It won't be proper New Year's Eve if you don't melt lead,' he said.

He told us that you could find out what would happen next year if you melted lead and poured it into cold water. If the lead set hard in a coin shape, for example, that meant you would get a lot of money next year. He let us borrow a little scoop too, the kind the boys usually have when they make toy soldiers at Grandad's.

We didn't tell the boys that Grandad had given us the lead.

Oh, we had so much fun that evening! My room was looking very nice. I had taken out all the rag rugs and beaten them, and dusted everywhere, and I had a lovely candlestick with five candles in it. I stood that in the middle of the table, and round it I put the bowl of apples, the juniper berry cordial and the bowl of nuts. When Britta and Anna arrived the candles were alight and looking so beautiful. I had a fire burning in the fireplace too.

'Welcoming in the New Year is something I like doing very much,' said Anna.

Lasse and Bosse and Olle were welcoming in the New Year in the boys' room. Between their room and mine is the big, dark attic. We had only just started our party when we heard padding feet outside in the attic. A moment later we heard an enormous bang, but we didn't pay any attention to it. We knew it was the boys trying to lure us out into the attic. We had heard Lasse's bangers before.

But then nothing else happened, so we started to get curious. We opened the door a crack and peered out. It was perfectly quiet and dark out there, so we decided to tiptoe across the attic and peep through the boys' keyhole to see what they were doing.

'I can't see anything,' said Britta, who looked first. 'They're not there.'

'It wouldn't surprise me if they'd decided to go to bed and sleep through it all,' said Anna.

'Well, that's a nice way to see in the New Year, I don't think,' I said. 'Come on, let's go in and get one of Lasse's bangers and wake them up.'

Bang! it went, right behind us. We nearly jumped out of our skin, we were so scared.

'Those twits have hidden themselves somewhere in the attic!' shouted Anna.

I ran to get my torch and we began to shine it in every corner and behind clothes and old boxes. But there were no boys to be seen.

'Well, that's very peculiar,' said Britta.

Bang! it went again, right behind us. It was another banger. We almost started to believe the attic was haunted.

'Just wait until I get hold of Lasse,' said Britta. 'I'll teach him a lesson or two.'

'Go right ahead,' we heard Lasse's voice say, high above our heads.

And there on the beams under the roof stood Lasse and Bosse and Olle. That made us so cross.

'So how's your stupid New Year party going?' said Lasse.

'Very well, thank you,' we said. 'We're just about to start melting lead to find out what will happen next year.'

Well, that certainly made them interested. They followed us into my room and when they saw how lovely we had made it look in there, with the candles and the fire and everything, they decided to come over and welcome in the New Year with us. Bosse ran to fetch their apples and nuts and juniper berry cordial.

Then we melted the lead in the scoop over the fire, and then each of us poured some into the water in my washing basin. Lasse poured his in first. When his lump of lead had set solid he lifted it out and looked closely at it. Then he said:

'It looks like I'm going to be king because this is a king's crown.'

'Ha ha!' laughed Anna. 'Can't you see it's a book! That means you'll be going to school all next year.'

My lump of lead looked very odd.

'I think it looks like a bicycle,' said Olle.

That made me ever so happy because I've been longing for a bicycle so much.

After everyone had finished doing their pieces of lead we sat on the floor in front of the fire and told stories. I think Britta tells such good stories. We ate lots of apples and nuts, and drank juniper cordial. And we played the nutting game. Britta and Anna knew a very good way to play nutting. It went like this:

First Britta said:

'Smoke's blowing in from the chimney!' And Anna answered:

'Then I'm running up to the attic!' And then Britta asked:

'How many boys are you taking with you?'

'Five,' said Anna, and because Britta had exactly five nuts in her hand she had to give them to Anna, because Anna had won that nutting round. Then we played the nutting game in lots of different ways, and Anna did so well that by the time we were finished she had twice as many nuts as anyone else.

All of a sudden Bosse began to yawn loudly and then he said he thought he'd lie down on my bed to welcome in the New Year. So he did. But two minutes later he was asleep. Mum and Dad came up and said goodnight to us, because they weren't going to stay up and welcome in the New Year.

We asked Lasse what the time was.

'Half past ten,' he said.

New Year's Eve night is longer than other nights, it seems to me. I thought it would never be midnight. But at last it was. We tried to wake Bosse, but it was absolutely impossible. We blew out the candles and stood by the window and looked out into the dark night to see the New Year coming. But we didn't see anything. After that we drank juniper berry cordial and shouted:

'Happy New Year!'

And we decided we would stay up and welcome in the New Year every year, because it was such fun. After that, all I wanted to do was go to sleep. But there in my bed was Bosse. We all took hold of his arms and legs and struggled with him over to his own bed. And even then he didn't wake up. Lasse undressed Bosse and put his nightshirt on. Then he tied one of my hair ribbons in Bosse's hair.

'It can stay there until tomorrow, so Bosse can see how much fun he had welcoming in the New Year,' said Lasse.

We Go to a Party at Auntie Jenny's

The best thing about the Christmas holidays was the party at Auntie Jenny's. My mum's sister Jenny lives on a farm far away on the other side of Storby Village. All of us Noisy Village children were invited to her house one Sunday after Christmas. We had to travel in the sleigh for hours and hours to get there.

Mum woke us up very early and wrapped us in layers of jumpers and scarves. I was sure I would suffocate before I got to the party, and even then Mum came rushing up with an extra shawl to wrap around my head. I said that if I was going to arrive at Auntie Jenny's looking like a spectacle then I wouldn't go with them.

We travelled in our wicker sleigh. Dad sat at the front, driving the horses. He had big straw shoes over his boots to keep his feet warm. Our sleigh went first, and behind us came South Farm's sleigh and last of all came North Farm's sleigh. Oh, how beautiful the bells on the horses sounded! We were so happy we started singing, but Mum said we had to stop that because otherwise we would breathe in too much cold air. But we shouted lots of things to Olle who was in the sleigh behind ours. And he shouted in turn to Britta and Anna.

'If they give us herring salad then I'm going home,' shouted Lasse.

'Me too,' shouted Olle.

Then he had to explain to Britta and Anna what he was shouting about. And in a while Olle shouted to us that Britta and Anna said they would also go home if we were given herring salad.

But we didn't go home even though we *were*

given herring salad, because there were a thousand other dishes to eat so we didn't have to take any herring salad.

Auntie Jenny has three girls, so there were masses of children at the party. We were up in a large room on the second floor and we played there all day, apart from when we had to eat. In the end we got so annoyed with all that food because as soon as we had started a game, Auntie came up to tell us that we had to go downstairs and eat something. I'm sure grown-ups do *nothing* but eat when they go to a party.

Auntie Jenny's oldest girl is called Nanna. We pretended that Nanna was a witch who lived in a wardrobe just outside the room where we were playing. In our game the wardrobe was her cottage and the room was a huge forest. As we were walking in the forest, picking berries, she came rushing out from her cottage and captured us. Oh, I was so afraid! I knew all the time that it was only Nanna, but I was just as scared as if it had been a real witch. There was a big wooden box in the wardrobe and we pretended it was the witch's oven and that she roasted Lasse in the oven. But he managed to get away at the last second, luckily.

'But I do smell a bit burnt,' said Lasse.

Sometimes the witch came running in shouting: 'Freeze!'

And that meant everyone had to stand absolutely still and not move a muscle. Once, when the witch shouted 'Freeze!' Lasse looked so ridiculous. He stood on one leg and stuck out his tongue and pulled out his ears and looked cross-eyed. This is what he looked like:

He had to stand still and look silly like that until the witch came and freed him from her spell. Oh, how we laughed at him!

Auntie Jenny's girls had a lovely dolls' house standing in one corner of the room. Anna and I couldn't help going over every so often to have a look. There was a kitchen and a dining room and a bedroom and a best room in the dolls' house, and a very grand family lived there. Nanna said they were called Duke and Duchess Candlesnuff. And they had a pretty little girl too, who sat on a chair in the best room. She was called Isabella Candlesnuff.

When the grown-ups had finally finished eating they came upstairs and they played too. We all played blind man's buff. Olle's dad was the blind man, and he had a large checked handkerchief tied over his eyes. We ran and tugged at his jacket as often as we could without getting caught. Then we played forfeits. I handed over my little gold heart, and to get it back I had to do a forfeit, which was three forward rolls. I did that, and then I was given my gold heart back. Olle's forfeit was to call the name of his sweetheart up the chimney. And, what a surprise, he called out 'Lisa!'. Lasse started to laugh, and I was awfully embarrassed. But then Olle looked jokingly at me and he said:

'I meant my mum, didn't you know that? She's called Lisa too.'

Dad had to pay his forfeit by jumping around the room like a frog. Oh, how we laughed at him! I've never seen Dad jump like a frog before. But the worst forfeit of all was the one Auntie Jenny had to do. She was told to climb up onto the table and stand on one leg and crow like a cockerel. But she didn't want to.

'Nonsense,' she said. 'That table won't take my weight, a fat old woman like me!'

And she was probably right, because Auntie Jenny weighs practically a hundred kilos.

We played for ages and had such a nice time. But Anna and I couldn't help sneaking over to the dolls' house every so often to say hello to Isabella Candlesnuff.

The best thing about the party at Auntie Jenny's was that we were going to sleep there overnight. I like having sleepovers in different places. Everything feels so unusual and special. It doesn't smell a bit like it does at home. There were fourteen of us children at the party and we all had to sleep next to our brothers and sisters in a long row on the floor in the room where we had been playing. Do you know, it's such fun sleeping on the floor! We had straw mattresses but no sheets, only blankets. When we had got into bed all the grown-ups came in to look at us.

'Look, here we have the youth of Sweden by the metre,' said Dad.

When they had gone we were supposed to be going to sleep, but it's probably almost impossible for fourteen youngsters to keep quiet. Nanna told us about a hoard of treasure that a knight had buried a long, long time ago, very close by. Lasse wanted to go out and dig for it in the very middle of night, but Nanna said no one was able to find it because it was enchanted treasure. Then I fell asleep.

We didn't leave for home until late next afternoon. It was completely dark by the time we arrived back in Noisy Village. We didn't shout anything to each other on the journey home because we were so tired. I lay back in the sleigh and looked up at all the stars. There were lots and lots and they were very far away. I crept further under the sheepskin rug and sang silently to myself, so that Lasse and Bosse wouldn't hear me:

'Twinkle, Twinkle, little star,

How I wonder what you are.'

I hope we can ride to Auntie Jenny's for a Christmas party next year as well.

Lasse Tumbles into the Lake

If you run right across North Farm's cow meadow you reach a small lake. That's where we go skating in winter. This year the lake was covered with such thick, smooth, hard ice. One day Mum didn't want us to go to the lake because Dad and Uncle Erik had made a big hole in the ice. They had cut out blocks of ice to store in our ice cellar. I said:

'But we'll see the juniper bushes they've put round the hole, so we'll be able to keep away from it.'

Then we were allowed to go.

Sometimes Lasse is rather stupid, usually when he's trying to make himself seem important. He did that now. He started skating as close to the hole in the ice as he could.

'Here comes the champion skater from Noisy Village,' he shouted. And he skated directly towards the hole and didn't swerve aside until the very last minute.

'Honestly Lasse, you're acting like an idiot,' said Olle.

We all told Lasse off, but that didn't help. He began skating in loops and swirls around the hole. Sometimes he skated backwards.

'Here he comes now, the magnificent skater from Noisy Village,' he yelled over and over again.

He came skating along all right—straight past and backwards into the hole with a splash, because he had come too close to the edge. We screamed. Lasse screamed too, worse than anyone. We were very frightened and thought Lasse would drown. Then we lay down on the ice in a long line, holding onto each other's feet. Bosse was at the front, by the hole, and we held tight, tight, onto his feet. And so Bosse pulled

Lasse up out of the hole, and we ran home as fast as we could. Lasse was *almost* crying, but not quite.

'What if you had come home drownded,' said Bosse.

'It's not called drownded, stupid,' said Lasse crossly. But he must have liked Bosse anyway, for pulling him out, because a little later that afternoon he gave Bosse a whole load of toy soldiers.

Mum was pretty angry with Lasse for tumbling through the hole in the ice. He was made to go to bed and drink hot milk to warm himself up. And after that he had to stay there for several hours. To think about the error of his ways, said Mum. That was when he gave Bosse the toy soldiers.

Anyhow, that evening we built a snow fort in the garden and had a snowball fight, and Lasse joined in, of course. Britta and Anna and I had one fort, and the boys had another. But the boys always make such hard snowballs and throw so hard too. That's unfair, I think. They came storming up to our fort with their hands full of snowballs, and Lasse shouted:

'To battle and victory! Here comes the Terror of the North!'

And Britta said:

'Oh really? I thought it was the champion skater from Noisy Village.'

Lasse didn't say anything after that for quite a long time.

The boys captured our fort and made us their prisoners, and said we had to make snowballs for them all evening otherwise we would die a death.

'What do you want all those snowballs for?' asked Anna.

'To save for midsummer, because there are never enough of them then,' answered Lasse.

'Oh, go and jump in the lake again,' said Anna.

Then Britta and Anna and I went to the barn because we were cold. In there it was lovely and warm. We played chase, and it wasn't long before the boys joined us. The cows glared at us. I don't think cows understand why you play chase. When I think about it, I don't really understand either. But it's good fun, it really is.

Dad came in soon after. He said we couldn't

play chase any longer because one of the cows was going to have a calf, and there mustn't be any disturbance. It was Lotta who was having the calf. We stayed and watched. Dad had to help the calf come out. It was a little bull calf, and he was so sweet. Lotta licked him and looked so proud. Dad said we could help him find a name for the calf.

'Terror of the North,' said Lasse. It seems he can't think of anything except his old Terror of the North. Such a stupid name for a sweet little calf!

'He could turn out to be an angry, dangerous bull when he grows up,' said Lasse.

Olle suggested the calf should be called Petter, and Dad thought that was a good suggestion.

'Well, he could at least be called Petter of the North,' said Lasse.

Then we ran to Grandad and told him that Lotta had a new calf.

Then it was bedtime. And just as Lasse and Bosse and I were standing outside our bedrooms, Lasse said:

'Heh, heh, heh, what a good job I'm not drownded after all.'

'Oh, go and jump in the lake,' said Bosse.

We Go Back to
School and Play
a Joke on Our Teacher

hen the Christmas holidays came to
an end it was still good weather for
sledging, so we went to school on
our kick sledges. We had three kick sledges.
Sometimes we put them together in one long
kick sledge with lots of places to sit.

Our teacher said it was lovely to see us again.
I thought it was lovely to see her too. She is so
kind. She offered all the children sweets because
it was the first day back. The sweets had been

bought in Stockholm. Our teacher had been there over the Christmas holidays. That was the only time I had ever eaten sweets bought in Stockholm.

It was good fun seeing all the children from Storby Village too. At break we swap bookmarks—well, not the boys, of course. In our class there's a girl called Anna-Greta. She's got so many bookmarks. During the first break after the Christmas holidays I swapped bookmarks with her. She got a basket of flowers and an elf from me, and I got a princess from her. It was practically the most beautiful bookmark I have ever seen. So I made a good swap, I think.

The boys generally have a snowball fight at break time in the winter. In the spring they play marbles. We play hopscotch. When boys don't have anything else to do they fight. And during lessons they get up to a whole lot of mischief. Our teacher says she thinks the boys get the fidgets and they can't stop themselves getting up to mischief. I think Lasse must get the fidgets an awful lot. Guess what he did once? He had been given a funny little pig as a Christmas present from Bosse. It was made of rubber and you could blow it up. Then when you let the air out, the pig squealed loudly. One day Lasse brought the pig to school with him. Lasse isn't in the same year as me, but because there are no more than 23 children in the whole school, we all sit in the same classroom. There is only one classroom, and only one teacher.

So that's how I know about the pig. Our class was doing reading. That's the best subject in school, I think, and it was my turn to read. It was all about a Swedish king called Gustav Vasa.

'Then the king burst into tears,' I read. And as soon as I had said that, there was a really sad squealing noise, almost enough to make you think it was Gustav Vasa himself who was squealing. But it wasn't. It was the pig in Lasse's desk. Lasse had reached under his desk and taken out the plug that sat in one end of the pig, and the air had come out. All the children giggled. Our teacher looked as if she wanted to giggle as well, but she didn't. Lasse had to stand in the naughty corner for the whole lesson. So did the pig.

But Lasse isn't the only one who causes trouble. All the boys are more or less the same. Once our teacher had to go to a meeting and we had to sit on our own and do sums and drawing. Our teacher told Britta to sit at the front at the teacher's desk while she was away. That's because Britta is so clever at school.

But no sooner had our teacher stepped outside the classroom than the boys started making a noise.

'Miss, Miss!' they all shouted, and waved their hands at Britta.

'What do you want?' asked Britta.

'We want to go outside,' they all shouted. And one boy, called Stig, waved his hand and yelled:

'Miss, Miss, how many steaks are there in a beef cow?'

And Bosse said:

'Have you heard how well the potatoes are growing this year, Miss?'

'Yes, actually I have heard that.'

And so Bosse said:

'Then you must have awfully good hearing, Miss!'

Lasse put up his hand and asked if he could show her what he had drawn, and he walked up to Britta with his drawing pad. But the whole pad was covered in black paint.

'And what is this supposed to be?' asked Britta.

'It's supposed to be five black cats down a coal mine.'

Britta thought being a teacher was no fun at all. She was glad when our real teacher came back. Our teacher asked her if the children had been good. And Britta said:

'Not the boys.'

So our teacher told the boys off and said they all had to stay behind after school and do arithmetic for a whole hour. And do you know what? At break time that boy Stig went up to Britta and said 'Tell-tale, tell-tale,' and bashed her on the head with his school bag. That was unfair, wasn't it?

As we were walking home Britta told me that she never wanted to be a teacher again in her entire life.

We dawdled as much as we could on the way

home so that Lasse and Bosse and Olle would have time to catch up with us. If they had come home a whole hour after us Mum would probably have wondered why, and then the boys would have had another telling-off. We thought the telling-off they got from our teacher was more than enough.

Once we had such fun at school. It was April the first and we played a trick on our teacher, which is what you *should* do on April the first. Well, perhaps not exactly should do, but you're allowed to do it, and you don't get punished for it.

Normally we start school at eight in the morning, but the day before April the first all of us children decided we would get to school at six o'clock the next day. There is a clock on the wall in our classroom. Just before our teacher locked the door of the classroom at the end of the last lesson, Lasse ran in and moved the hands of the clock forward two hours.

The following day we all got to school at six o'clock. But the clock on the wall said eight o'clock, of course.

We stamped our feet and thumped about as

loudly as we could so that our teacher would hear us. She lives in the schoolhouse on the floor above the classroom.

Lasse ran up the stairs and knocked on her door. And our teacher said sleepily:

'Who is it?'

'It's Lasse,' said Lasse. 'Isn't there going to be any school today?'

'Oh, you poor child, I've overslept,' said our teacher. 'I'll be with you any minute.'

Naturally our teacher has a clock where she lives but I expect she was in such a hurry that she didn't have time to look at it.

When the clock in the classroom said twenty past eight our teacher came and let us in.

'I don't understand why my alarm clock hasn't rung and woken me up,' she said. 'It's very annoying.'

Oh, it was hard for us not to laugh. The first lesson was arithmetic, and right in the middle of working out some sums we heard our teacher's alarm clock go off upstairs, because then it really was seven o'clock. But the clock in the classroom said nine.

'What *is* going on?' said our teacher, astonished.

'April Fool, April Fool! The trick we played is best of all!' we all shouted.

You can only say that to your teacher on April the first.

'Oh, such children,' said our teacher.

When all the lessons on the timetable were over we thought we would be allowed to go

home, of course, even though the clock showed one o'clock. But then our teacher said:

'April Fool, April Fool, you stay another hour in school!'

So we had to stay for one more hour. But that didn't matter, because our teacher read some funny stories to us.

On the way home Olle suddenly said to Lasse:

'Oh Lasse, you've got a great big hole in the

back of your trousers!'

Lasse almost twisted his head off trying see the hole, and after he had been doing it for a while, Olle said:

'April Fool!'

Olle was overjoyed that he had been able to trick Lasse. Then a moment later we met the nasty shoemaker who lives halfway between Storby Village and Noisy Village. Olle was so full of the joke he had played on Lasse that he said:

'Look, Mr Gentle, there's a fox in the bushes!'

But Mr Gentle didn't look at the bushes. Instead he replied:

'And here comes a gaggle of geese walking along the road, I see.'

Lasse laughed at that.

In the afternoon, after we had done our homework, Lasse ran off to South Farmhouse and said to Olle:

'Olle, a scrap metal man has come to North Farm. He's buying up stones.'

'He's buying stones?' said Olle, who had completely forgotten it was April the first. 'What kind of stones?'

'The kind of stones you've got here in your garden,' replied Lasse.

So Olle started picking up stones and putting them in a sack, as many as he could carry, and he staggered off to North Farmhouse with the sack. There really was a man there, but he was only buying empty bottles and old junk.

'Here you are, mister, more stones,' said Olle. He held out the sack to the man and looked very pleased with himself.

'Stones?' said the man. He didn't understand a thing. 'Did you say stones?'

'Yes,' said Olle, looking even more pleased with himself. 'First class grey stones, they are. I've collected them myself from our garden.'

'I see,' said the man. 'Well, you've been tricked proper, you have, little fellow.'

Then Olle remembered that it was April the first. His face went bright red and he picked up his sack and dragged it home without saying a word. But Lasse stood behind the fence and shouted 'April Fool, April Fool!' so that all of Noisy Village could hear.

Easter in Noisy Village

N ow I'm going to tell you what it was like last Easter here in Noisy Village.

On the Wednesday before Easter, Britta and Anna came to see me early in the morning because we were going to make Holy Wednesday tickets, those bits of paper you pin onto people's backs when they're not looking. We do that when it's Easter. We dress up as little old witches and fly to Blue Hilltop, and you need a ticket to get in. We cut out masses of white paper squares and painted funny figures on them. On some of them we wrote 'Angry orangutan' and 'Watch out for the dog' and things like that. There was a lot of commotion going on in Lasse and Bosse's room. The boys were making Holy Wednesday tickets, too. Olle was there, helping.

When we had filled our pockets full of Holy Wednesday tickets Britta and Anna and me went in to Lasse and Bosse and Olle and asked if we could all go out and play. That was only because we wanted to pin Holy Wednesday tickets on them.

We ran over to North Farm, to the place where they saw the timber. We climbed about on the piles of planks. All the time we tried to get close enough to each other to pin on the tickets, but it didn't work very well because everyone was careful not to turn their back on anyone. Soon Agda, who helps our mum at home, came along to tell us it was time to go home and eat. Immediately, Lasse leaped down from the pile of planks and ran to catch up with Agda. He walked beside her, talking as fast as he could, and without Agda noticing he pinned a Holy Wednesday ticket on to her back. 'Oh how I like

Oskar' it said on the piece of paper. Oskar is our farmhand. When he came into the kitchen to eat, Agda was walking around with the words 'Oh how I like Oskar' on her back. Oskar slapped his knees and laughed and said:

'That's good, Agda dear. That's good.'

Lasse and Bosse and I laughed even louder. Eventually Agda realized that it was Holy Wednesday and felt her back, where she found the ticket and threw it into the kitchen stove. But she laughed too.

After we had eaten I managed to pin one of the tickets on Lasse's jacket which was hanging over the back of a chair. He put on his jacket and didn't notice a thing, so when we got back to where the planks were, Lasse was climbing about with a big white ticket on his back. It said: 'What a pity I'm so stupid.' Oh, how we laughed! Lasse, who always said that no one would ever, ever be able to pin any Holy Wednesday tickets on him!

Next day was Maundy Thursday and that evening all of us children dressed up as Easter witches, even the boys. I wore Agda's checked scarf on my head and a striped apron and a long, black skirt, and I took the long rake we use for getting the ashes out of the stove and used it as a broomstick to ride on. Lasse had the long broom from the barn. I rode over to North Farmhouse to leave an Easter letter that I had written for Britta and Anna. 'Happy Easter wishes to you from an old witch who is flying off to Blue Hilltop now' the letter said.

Dad was burning leaves in our garden and all of us Easter witches ran around him, jumping over piles of smoking leaves, pretending we were on Blue Hilltop. Anna and I agreed that soon we would go and see if the blue wood anemones had begun to poke out of the ground in our special place behind the outhouse.

On Easter Saturday Mum and Dad were going to a party at the Vicarage in Storby Village, and so Lasse and Bosse and I were allowed to invite Olle and Britta and Anna to our house for an egg party. Mum runs the chicken farm in Noisy Village so we have lots of eggs. Bosse thinks Albertina lays most of the eggs. Albertina is Bosse's own hen.

'You seem to think Albertina can shoot out eggs like a machine gun,' said Lasse to Bosse.

We ate in the kitchen. The table was laid so prettily with a blue cloth and our yellow Easter plates. We had birch twigs as well, in a vase. Lasse and Bosse and I had painted all the eggs red and yellow and green. Eggs should always look like that, I think, because it looks so nice. We had written rhymes on the eggs too.

'Anna this is for you, instead of potatoes and stew,' it said on one egg. Lasse had written that, but Bosse said it was a rotten verse.

'No one thought of giving her potatoes and stew anyway,' said Bosse.

'You don't know what these eggs are instead of,' answered Lasse. '"Anna this is for you, instead of a sock and a shoe". Do you think that would have been better?'

No, Bosse didn't think so. And we didn't have time to change the rhyme in any case, because just then Britta and Anna and Olle turned up. We had so much fun while we sat there eating. We had a competition to see who could eat the most eggs. I could only manage three, but Olle ate six.

'Albertina is a good hen,' said Bosse, when we had finished. Afterwards we were going to hunt for our Easter eggs filled with sweets. Mum had hidden them before she left. Lasse and Bosse and I usually have a great big egg every Easter, with lots and lots of sweets inside, but this year Mum said that if we were happy to have smaller eggs, she could buy an egg each for Britta and Anna and Olle too. We could have them as a surprise at our Easter party. And of course that's what we wanted. Mum had hidden the eggs very cleverly. Mine was in the cupboard where we keep the saucepans. It was silver with little flowers on. Oh, it was so pretty! There was a chicken made of marzipan inside it, and masses of sweets.

We could stay up precisely as long as we wanted, because it was Easter Saturday. Agda was out walking with Oskar, so we were completely alone in the whole house. We switched off all the lights everywhere and played Hide and Seek in the dark. We did 'Eeny meeny miny moe, catch a tiger by the toe' and it was Bosse who went first. Oh, what a good hiding place I found! I climbed up onto the window sill in the sitting room and hid behind the curtains. Bosse tiptoed up and down several times very close to me, but he didn't see me. But I think the very best hiding place of the whole evening was the one Britta found. Out in the porch stood Dad's wellington boots, and hanging above them was the overcoat he wears when he drives the cows to the dairy in the mornings. Britta stepped into the boots and wrapped the coat around her. In the end we turned on the light and we all searched for her, shouting 'Come out, come out, wherever you are!', but she only stood there, quiet as a mouse. And although we looked in every single place, we still couldn't find her. Dad's boots and coat looked exactly the same as usual. How could we know that Britta was inside?

'Perhaps she's dead and gone,' said Olle.

But then we heard giggling coming from inside the coat and Britta stepped out, still wearing Dad's big boots. She wanted us to play that she was Puss in Boots, but Anna wanted us to go to Grandad and make egg toddy.

We went to Grandad's. We took with us eggs, sugar and ice cream. Grandad was sitting in his rocking chair in front of the fire and he was so happy to see us. We sat on the floor in front of the fire and stirred the egg toddy so hard it splashed all over the place. Anna stirred for Grandad, because he is almost blind and can't do it for himself. Grandad told us what it was like in the old days. In those days children didn't get any Easter eggs with sweets in. I told Grandad that my Easter egg was silver with little flowers on, because he couldn't see it, of course.

I think it's so much fun to hear Grandad tell us what it was like in the old days. Do you know, one Easter when Grandad was little, it was so cold that his dad had to use a poker to smash the ice on the water bucket that stood in their kitchen. Wasn't that awful? And no Easter eggs, either! Poor children.

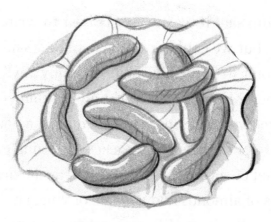

Anna and
I Go Shopping

The shop where we buy sugar and coffee and things like that is in Storby Village, very near our school. When Mum needs things at home, it's usually me who has to buy them for her after school. But one day during the Easter holidays Mum had run out of a few things and she said to me:

'Lisa, it can't be helped, you'll have to run to the shop for me.'

It was such lovely weather that I thought it would be fun to go shopping. So I said:

'All right, then! What do you want me to get?'

Mum said it was probably best to write it all down, but we couldn't find a pen. So I said:

'Don't worry, I'll remember it anyway!'

Then Mum started to list all the things I had to buy: twenty grams of yeast and half a dozen of the best pork sausages, a packet of ground ginger, a packet of sewing needles, a tin of anchovies, 100 grams of almonds and a bottle of vinegar.

'Yes, I'm sure I'll remember everything,' I said.

At that very moment Anna came skipping into our kitchen, asking if I wanted to go with her to the shop.

'Ha ha!' I laughed. 'I was just coming to ask you.'

Anna had her new red hat on and a basket over her arm. So I put my new green hat on and a basket over my arm too.

Anna had to buy soap and a packet of crispbread and half a kilo of coffee and a kilo of sugar lumps and two metres of elastic. And she was to get half a dozen of the best pork sausages as well, just like me. Anna hadn't written down what she was supposed to buy, either.

Before we left we dashed up to Grandad to see if there was anything he wanted from the shop, and Grandad asked us to buy some barley sugar sweets for him, and a bottle of camphor liniment for his aches and pains.

Just as we were standing outside the gate, Olle's Mum came running down their front steps.

'Are you going to the shop?' she shouted.

'Yes,' we said.

'Oh, would you be kind and buy a few things for me?' she asked.

We said we would be happy to. She wanted us to buy a reel of white sewing thread and a little tub of vanilla sugar.

'Oh, wait, what else was I going to have?' she asked, looking puzzled.

'Half a dozen of the best pork sausages?' I suggested.

'Yes, that's exactly what it was,' said Olle's mum. 'How did you guess?'

Then Anna and I set off, feeling a bit worried that we wouldn't be able to remember everything. First we went through the list of things, taking it in turns, but we got tired of doing that. Then we walked arm in arm, swinging our baskets, and the sun shone and the trees smelled lovely. We sang as loudly as we could. 'Half a dozen of the best pork sausages,' we sang. It sounded really good. This is how we did it: first I sang 'best pork sausages' to a beautiful slow tune, and then Anna came in with 'of the very best, of the very best', very fast and cheerfully. Sometimes we sang to a tune that was good for marching, but in the end we settled for one that was very gloomy but incredibly beautiful from beginning to end. It almost made us want to cry.

'Oh, how sad sausages are,' said Anna, when we finally arrived at the shop.

There were a lot of people inside so we had to wait for a long time before it was our turn. Actually, we had to wait even longer, because it seems that adults think children can wait forever in shops. They always push themselves in front. But finally old Emil himself came into the shop. We know him. He started asking us how everything was in Noisy Village, and if we had eaten a lot of eggs over Easter, and if we were thinking of getting married soon.

'We're certainly not thinking of doing *that,*' we said.

'And what can I do for you ladies today?' asked Emil.

He always talks in a silly way like that, but I like him anyway. He has a pen behind his ear and

a small red moustache, and he always offers us sour sweets that he keeps in a big jar.

First Anna told him everything she had to buy for her mum and for Grandad. Emil weighed things out and wrapped them up as Anna said them one by one.

Then it was my turn to tell him everything I had to buy for my Mum and for Olle's mum. Both me and Anna thought really hard to make sure we didn't forget anything. Then Emil gave us some sour sweets and we left.

We had just passed the school when we met a boy we know. He saw that we were wearing new hats.

After we had walked on for a bit and had reached the place where the road to Noisy Village turns off, I said:

'Anna, do you remember if I bought any yeast?'

But Anna couldn't remember at all. We started squeezing the parcels in my basket, but there was nothing that felt like yeast. So we had to turn back to the shop. Old Emil laughed at us and gave us the yeast and some sour sweets.

Then we left.

We had just got to the turning in the road again when Anna yelled out:

'Oh, Grandad's camphor liniment!'

'Well, would you believe it!' I said.

There was nothing for it but go back to the shop again. Oh, how Emil laughed at us! He gave us the camphor liniment and even more sour sweets.

When we reached the turning in the road again, Anna looked so horrified that I really felt sorry for her.

'Lisa,' she said. 'I'm almost certain I haven't bought any sugar.'

'Anna,' I said. 'Don't tell me you haven't bought sugar. Surely to *goodness* you bought sugar!'

We prodded and prodded the things in Anna's basket, but there was nothing that felt sugar-like in the least.

Old Emil almost fell over backwards behind the counter when he saw us again. But he gave us the sugar. And even more sour sweets.

'I think I'd better get out a new jar of sweets

to have in reserve,' he said. 'It looks like I'm going to get through my entire stock.'

'No, we won't be coming back any more,' said Anna.

Just before we reached the turning in the road again, I said:

'Anna, let's *run* past it. It's the only way. Otherwise we'll remember something else we have forgotten.'

So we ran past the fork in the road.

'Well, that went all right,' said Anna.

At last we were on the way home. Oh, it was such a lovely day, one of the first warm spring days. We walked arm in arm and swung our baskets, although not too much or else everything would have fallen out. The sun was shining and the forest smelled lovely.

'Let's sing again for little while,' said Anna.

So we did. We started on 'Half a dozen sausages of the very best kind'. It sounded quite as beautiful as before and Anna said we ought to tell them about that song at school and sing it on the last day of term.

We sang and we sang and we sang as we

struggled up the hills towards Noisy Village.

And then, just as I was yelling out 'Half a dozen sausages' extra beautifully, Anna grabbed my arm and looked absolutely shocked.

'Lisa,' she said. 'We haven't *bought* any sausages!'

We sat down at the roadside and said nothing for a long time. Then Anna said that she wished sausages had never been invented.

'Why can't people eat meatballs instead?' she said.

'We should never have run past the turning in the road,' I said.

We had to go back. It couldn't be helped.

Ugh, it was horrible. We didn't sing any more. Anna said she didn't think the song about sausages was at all suitable to sing on the last day of term.

'No,' I said. 'Not on the last day of term and not on any other day either. It's an absolutely ridiculous song!'

When Emil caught sight of us again, he clasped his forehead and ran to get the new jar of sour sweets. But we said no thanks, we didn't want any more sweets.

'No?' said Emil. 'Then what *do* you want?'

'Three lots of half a dozen pork sausages of the very best kind,' we said.

'If there are sausages that are any good, that is,' muttered Anna.

We dragged ourselves homewards. When we reached the turning in the road Anna looked behind her and said:

'Look! Here comes Johan the Miller on his cart with his ugly old grey mare!'

Johan lives at the flour mill on the other side of Noisy Village.

'Can you give us a lift?' we shouted, as Johan came alongside us.

'Course I can,' said Johan.

We jumped up in the cart behind Johan and travelled all the way home to Noisy Village. Once I begun humming 'Half a dozen pork sausages of the very best kind', but then Anna said:

'If you sing a single note of that tune I'll shove you off the cart.'

When I went into our kitchen to Mum, she

said: 'What an extremely long time you've been!'

'It's not surprising,' I said. 'When you have to buy so many sausages.'

When Mum had taken everything out of the basket she said:

'What a clever girl you are to remember everything.'

We See the
Water Spirit

The main road actually comes to an end at Noisy Village, but it carries on as a narrow, bumpy road through the forest to Johan the Miller. Johan is an odd little man. He lives all alone in a cottage in the middle of the forest, and right next to his cottage is the water mill. It stands beside a stream called Willow Brook. Willow Brook isn't one of those calm, gentle streams, like the one we've got at home in our meadow. Oh no. It comes roaring and rushing along very fast. Otherwise you couldn't have a mill there, of course, because the great big millstone wouldn't be able to turn if the water wasn't in such a hurry to get past and drive the mill wheel.

Not many people come to grind their flour at Johan's mill, only us Noisy Village people and a few others who live on the other side of the forest. So Johan spends a lot of time on his own over there at his mill. The odd thing is that Johan doesn't like grown-ups. He only likes children. When we go to Johan he talks non-stop, but if there are any grown-ups there he doesn't say a word, except if he has to answer questions.

One day last spring Dad told Lasse to drive over to the mill with a couple of sacks of rye that needed to be ground into flour.

'Oh good,' we all said. 'We'll come too.'

We have an old black mare called Svea. Dad has owned that mare for such a long time. He calls her his proposal mare. That's because when Dad drove off to ask Mum to marry him it was Svea who was pulling the cart. Dad isn't worried at all when we drive the cart with Svea. He says that Svea has more sense than all the Noisy Village children put together.

Two sacks of rye and all of us children, that was a heavy load. Svea turned her head to see and she did not look happy. But Lasse slapped the reins and said:

'Come on, Svea, don't be silly now!'

Off we set along the forest road. It certainly is stony and bumpy, that road, and we kept jolting into each other as the cart bounced over the stones. But that only made us laugh.

Long before you see the mill you can hear the rush of Willow Brook as you come driving through the forest. Oh, it's an exciting place, that mill! And it's very beautiful there. But it's a bit scary too. When you stand there looking at the mill wheel turning and want to say something, you practically have to shout to be heard.

Johan was very happy when we turned up. We followed him into the mill. He walked around chuckling all the time, and looking very pleased with himself. After we had left our sacks and looked at everything, we all sat in the grass outside the mill and Johan started talking. Probably he hadn't had anyone to talk to for days because he chatted worse than ever.

Johan says that a little elf lives inside the mill. Johan has seen him many times. Most of the time the elf is nice, but sometimes he gets up to mischief. Then he grabs hold of the millstone and holds it so it can't turn, or else he tips a whole sack of flour onto the floor. Once, when Johan came into the mill very, very early one morning, the elf smacked him on the head. All Johan saw was a kind of flash of lightning as he stepped through the door. Then the elf was gone, just like that. But mostly the elf is kind and sweeps the floor and keeps the mill tidy.

Yes, the mill is definitely a strange place. Behind Johan's cottage is an open glade among the trees, and that's where the fairies dance, says Johan. Johan usually sits in his room and spies on them from behind the curtains. If the fairies catch sight of Johan they disappear in an instant. Johan has also seen a wood nymph. She was standing behind a pine tree and she stuck her head round the tree trunk and laughed so it echoed all around the forest. Oh, I think Johan is lucky to have seen all of that.

We had heard about it many times before, of

course, but Johan told us again, while we were sitting there in the grass.

'But do you know who I saw last night?' said Johan. He was almost whispering.

No, how could we know that? Then Johan told us he had seen the water spirit.

Anna squeezed my hand, and I squeezed hers.

'And where exactly did you see the water spirit, Johan?' asked Lasse.

Then Johan said that he had been sitting on a stone in the stream directly below the mill pond, and he was playing his violin so beautifully that it made Johan cry. He couldn't help himself. Johan showed us the stone where the water spirit had been sitting, but sadly enough there was no water spirit sitting there now.

'He only shows himself at night-time,' said Johan.

'Does he come every night?' asked Bosse.

'Well, seems to me he plays like crazy in the springtime, sitting there in the dark,' said Johan.

Svea wanted us to go home now, that was plain. So we said goodbye to Johan. Anna and I ran to have another look at the stone where the water spirit had been sitting.

There is another narrow road which runs from the mill to the farms on the other side of the forest. Lasse came up with the idea that it would be fun to drive down and look at those farms, so he smacked his lips at Svea and tried to get her to start walking along that road. But do you know what, it was altogether impossible! Svea stood absolutely still and would not budge from the spot. All she did was turn her head and look at Lasse, as if she wanted to see if he was quite right in the head. So there was nothing for it but to drive back to Noisy Village. Oh, how fast Svea trotted on the way home!

All of a sudden Lasse said:

'I've decided to go to the mill tonight to look at the water spirit. Anyone want to come with me?'

At first we thought he was joking. But he wasn't. Then Bosse and Olle said they were also going to go and look at him.

'Good,' said Lasse. 'It really doesn't matter if the girls come or not.'

'And why shouldn't we come as well, may I

ask?' said Britta.

'Yes, that's what I say too,' said Anna.

'Okay with me,' said Lasse. 'It would be good for you to see a water spirit or two. You haven't seen that many in your lifetime.'

'Oh, and have *you* seen one, then?' asked Britta.

Lasse didn't answer that. He simply looked mysterious, as if he had seen dozens of water spirits.

Ooh, it was exciting! Lasse said we should set off at midnight. We planned it all while we were going along in the cart. Lasse thought it was best not to ask permission. He said grown-ups get such strange ideas when children want to go and see water spirits. It was better to ask for permission afterwards, said Lasse, just to be on the safe side.

Lasse has an old alarm clock and he promised to wake us all up. So in the middle of the night I was woken up by Lasse who was standing by my bed and pulling my hair. I shot out of bed.

In the evening, before we had gone to sleep, Lasse had made a device to wake up Britta and

Anna. He had tied a piece of string around a stone, put the stone on the floor in Britta and Anna's room, and then run the string in through my window. My room is right opposite Britta and Anna's room, and the houses are very close together. Now he started tugging on the string, making the stone thud up and down on the floor over at Britta and Anna's. And that woke them up.

Waking Olle was easy. All you have to do is climb through the linden tree that grows between South Farmhouse and Middle Farmhouse. The boys always go that way when they want to see each other.

I can't believe we did it. I was positive Mum and Dad would wake up, the way the stairs creaked as we crept out. But they didn't.

I would never in my life dare to walk through the forest alone at night, because it's totally different then to how it is in the daytime. I held very hard onto Britta and Anna as we walked along the road towards the mill. When we had come so close that we could hear the rushing stream, all I wanted to do most was run back home!

But Lasse was very sure of himself.

'Now we've got to sneak up one at a time to look at the water spirit,' he said.

'One at a time! No thanks, Lasse,' I said. 'I won't do it at all if I've got to go alone.'

'You are stupid,' said Lasse. 'We can't go in a long line like we're on a school outing and ask to have a look at him. I'm going to sneak up on my own, anyway.'

Olle and Bosse decided to sneak up together. And Britta and Anna and I were going to sneak up all three of us. But oh, how fast my heart was beating inside me!

'I'll go first and have a look,' said Lasse. 'If the water spirit isn't there I'll shout for you. Count to a hundred! If I haven't shouted by then, you can come after me, because that means he's here.'

So he crept off. Oh, I think he was so brave. We lay there in the moss and counted, and I *almost* hoped I would hear Lasse shout, because the closer we got to a hundred the faster my heart was beating. But we didn't hear a shout.

'That means the water spirit is there,' said Bosse. And so he and Olle crept off in one direction,

73

and Britta and Anna and me in another direction.

'I think I'm going to die,' said Anna.

Ooh, there was the mill! There was the mill pond! And there, oh, there was the stone! And he was sitting there! The water spirit was sitting there! He was stark naked. And he was playing music. It was quite hard to hear among the noise of all that rushing water, and you couldn't see him very clearly because it was so dark. But he was sitting there, he really was.

'Oh, I can see him,' whispered Anna.

'Listen to that,' whispered Britta.

'It doesn't sound like a violin,' I whispered. 'And what's that tune?'

'He . . . he's playing "Row, row, row your boat".'

'Well, who'd have thought it?' I said.

Yes, he really was playing "Row, row, row your boat". It was a very funny water spirit, I must say. And that water spirit was none other than Lasse, sitting on the stone and playing a mouth organ. Stark naked.

'At least now you've seen the water spirit,' said Lasse afterwards.

Bosse said that when he got a bit older he was going to give Lasse a good sorting out.

Olle Gets
a Sister

Sometimes I get so tired of Lasse and
Bosse and then I think it would be better
not to have any brothers at all. They
tease me when I play with my dolls. They box all
the time and are too rough. And they keep telling
me it's my turn to do the drying up. Once Lasse
asked Mum why they chose a girl—he didn't
understand the point of it. He said it would have
been much better to have nine boys, as well as
Lasse and Bosse, so you had enough for a football
team. But then Mum said:

'I'm so glad I've got my little girl. Nine boys?

Good heavens! It's more enough with you two rascals.'

So Lasse got nowhere with his stupid suggestion.

But sometimes I think it's good to have brothers. Like when we have pillow fights and when they come into my room and tell ghost stories, and when it's Christmas, and things like that. Once Bosse was so kind. There was a boy in school who whacked me just because I happened to bump into him and made him drop his books. But then Bosse whacked him and said:

'Don't do that again!'

'Why did she have to go and bump into me?' said Bengt. That was the boy's name.

'She couldn't help it. She didn't see you. Do you think she's got eyes in the back of her neck, stupid?' said Bosse.

Oh, I liked Bosse then! And Lasse and Bosse always give me sweets when they buy some. So really it isn't that bad having brothers. Though it would be better to have sisters, obviously.

'The main thing is to have *some* brothers or sisters,' says Olle. Before his baby sister came along he was always so cross because he didn't have any brothers or sisters.

'Other people get children, but here at our farm we never get any children,' Olle would say angrily.

But then he did get a sister, after all. And oh, how happy he was! The day she was born he came racing over to say we had to come and look at her that very minute. So we did.

'There she is,' said Olle, looking as if he was showing us an actual miracle. 'Isn't she sweet?' he said, and he looked absolutely delighted.

But actually she *wasn't*. She was all red and wrinkly—honestly, she looked revolting, I thought. Although her hands were quite sweet, really.

Never have I seen anyone look as surprised as Lasse did when he saw Olle's sister. His eyes widened and his mouth dropped open. But he didn't say anything. 'Yes, she's very pretty,' said Britta. And then we went out.

Afterwards Lasse said to Bosse:

'Poor Olle! Imagine having a sister like that! Not that Lisa is a beauty, but at least she looks like other people, more or less. Just think when that kid starts school! Olle will be so ashamed of her. There's never been an uglier girl at our school.'

Then almost a week passed and we didn't go to South Farmhouse at all. Olle talked every day about how sweet his sister was, and every time he did Lasse's face looked peculiar. But then we were all invited to South Farmhouse because Olle's sister was going to be christened.

'Oh, the poor child,' said Lasse. 'It's probably best for her if she dies young.'

The sitting room at South Farmhouse was looking lovely. There were lots of flowers everywhere because Olle's sister was born in the spring when there are cowslips and lily of the valley. There was a vase of birch branches standing in the fireplace, and the table was laid for coffee. And Olle was dressed in his best clothes. So were we, by the way. The vicar was standing there, waiting. And all of a sudden the door opened and Auntie Lisa came in with Olle's little sister in her arms. And oh, how sweet that child had become! She had large, dark blue eyes, her face was all pink, and as for her mouth, well, I can't tell you what a sweet little mouth she had!

And she was dressed in a beautiful, long white christening gown.

Lasse looked as surprised as when he saw her for the first time.

'Have you got a new one?' he whispered to Olle.

'A new what?' asked Olle.

'A new baby,' said Lasse.

'Don't tell me you've forgotten I had a sister,' said Olle, who hadn't a clue that Lasse thought it was a different child. Lasse didn't say anything else.

The vicar christened Olle's sister with the name Kerstin.

Oh, I like Kerstin so much! She is the sweetest baby there ever was. Anna and Britta and me dash over to South Farmhouse almost every day to watch Auntie Lisa look after her. You should see how she waves her arms and legs about. Kerstin I mean, not Auntie Lisa. It looks so cute. Sometimes Olle tries to copy her, but that doesn't look the tiniest bit cute. She waves her arms and legs about most when she is having a bath in the big bowl. She likes having a bath a lot. Sometimes, when she is lying in her bed, it's almost as if she is talking. It sounds like 'oodge, oodge'. Olle thinks she'll be able to say all sorts of things soon, but Auntie Lisa says it will be a while yet, because Kerstin is only five months old. When Olle goes up to Kerstin's cot and looks at her, she gives a big grin, precisely as if she is absolutely delighted to see him. She hasn't got any teeth, but it looks very sweet anyway when she laughs. Her eyes really shine at Olle when he looks at her. Svipp is a bit jealous of Kerstin. He only wants Olle to like *him*, of course. But then Olle pats Svipp over and over and tells him he is a lovely, good dog, and then Svipp isn't jealous any more.

One day Anna and I were allowed to look after Kerstin. Auntie Lisa was very busy doing the baking. Olle wasn't at home, luckily, otherwise he would have wanted to look after her. Oh, it was all so much fun! This is what happened. Kerstin was in her cot and screaming the house down, just when Auntie Lisa was making the bread. She was wet and hungry and cross. Kerstin, I mean, not Auntie Lisa. So Auntie Lisa said: 'Do you think you would be able to give her a bath?'

'Oh yes!' we shouted. That made us so happy.

Anna fetched the big bowl and poured in the water, but Auntie Lisa came and tested it with her elbow to make sure it wasn't too hot. I went and lifted Kerstin out of her cot. Do you know, she stopped screaming straight away and starting laughing instead. And when I held her close to me she bit my cheek. It didn't hurt. It felt nice, because she hasn't got any teeth, of course. It made my face all wet, but that didn't matter.

I know how to hold babies. You have to hold them so that their back is supported, so Auntie Lisa taught me. And I know how to hold them when you bath them too, so that whatever happens, their head doesn't go under the water. I held Kerstin and Anna washed her with the flannel. And Kerstin kicked her legs and arms and said 'Oodge, oodge'. She also tried to suck on the flannel, but I wasn't going to let *that* happen!

'She's so sweet you could eat her all up,' said Anna.

Anna had put the changing mat on the kitchen table with a towel on top to dry her with. I lay

Kerstin down on it very carefully when she had finished her bath. We wrapped the towel around her and dried her. We both helped to do that, Anna and me. Then we put baby powder all over her. Suddenly Kerstin stuck her big toe in her mouth and started sucking it. Oh, that looked handy! No one on this earth can have such cute toes as Kerstin. But we had to take her big toe away from her so we could put on her little vest and jumper. Then Auntie Lisa helped us to put her nappy on, because that was a bit more difficult. But we put her trousers on all by ourselves. Then she was completely ready and Auntie Lisa fed her.

Afterwards Anna and I were allowed to go out and push Kerstin in her pram. We pretended that Anna was the daddy and I was the mummy and Kerstin was our little baby. It wasn't long before Kerstin fell asleep, but we carried on pushing her, and it was lots of fun. Just as we were walking there Olle came along, on his way home. And immediately he ran up and took the pram from us, exactly as if he thought we were trying to kidnap Kerstin. But after he had pushed

Kerstin for a while he let us hold the handle too, and help push.

We told Olle that Kerstin had sucked her big toe, and Olle laughed happily and said:

'Oh yes, you wouldn't believe how many tricks that child can do. She might even be in a circus when she's bigger.'

He pushed for a while longer, and then he said:

'So she sucked her big toe, did she? Well, she always does that practically every day, but I'm glad you saw it, anyway.'

At that moment Kerstin woke up and saw Olle. He tickled her under the chin and said:

'So, you little monkey, did you suck your big toe?'

And he laughed again and looked even more pleased. Exactly as if sucking your big toe was the cleverest thing anyone could do in the whole world!

When it Rains

O ne morning, just after we had broken up for the summer holidays, I woke up in a bad mood. It wasn't a nice day at all. It was so rainy and windy you couldn't go out. And I had quarrelled with Britta and Anna. We had been playing hopscotch the day before, and Britta and Anna said I had stepped on the line, when I absolutely had not stepped on the line.

'If you're going to be so unfair then I don't want to play hopscotch with you any more,' I said.

'So what?' said Britta. 'No one's forcing you.'

'Yes, you can't have your own way all the time,' said Anna.

So I went home. Britta and Anna went on playing hopscotch for a long time. I stood behind the curtains in our kitchen and watched them, but I made very sure that they didn't see me. And I decided I would never, ever play with them again.

But oh, how bored I was when it rained the next day! I had no idea what to do at all.

Lasse and Bosse had bad colds and had been in their beds for three days. I went in to chat to them, but they were reading and only mumbled when I spoke to them. Actually, what I really wanted was to go and see what Britta and Anna were up to. Then I remembered how unfair they had been and I made up my mind never to go to North Farmhouse again in my entire life. Instead I went down to Mum in the kitchen.

'Oh Mum, everything is so boring,' I said.

'Is it?' said Mum. 'I hadn't noticed.'

'Yes, because all it does is rain and rain,' I said. 'I don't know what to do.'

'If I were you I would bake a sponge cake,' said Mum.

Mum said that exactly as if I *knew* how to bake a sponge cake. But I didn't. That is, I had never tried.

But guess what! I made a sponge cake all by myself, and very good it was too. Although Mum told me what to do, of course. This is what I did. First I whisked together two eggs and two coffee cups of sugar in a bowl. I whisked for a long time, and that was fun. Then I melted a big lump of butter in a saucepan and mixed it into the frothy mixture. Then I put in flour and milk. I don't remember exactly how much. I also put in grated lemon peel and baking powder.

While I was making the cake I wore a large white apron and white head scarf.

Oh, how exciting it was when Mum took my cake out of the oven! She tipped it out onto a clean tea towel and it was all light brown and spongy. I had no idea I was so good at making sponge cakes. Mum thought I should take some of my cake and some squash up to Lasse and Bosse. So I did. That made them very glad. And very surprised too, when I told them it was me who had made the cake.

Then I had an idea. It's true Britta and Anna had been unfair, but I thought perhaps I could forgive them and offer them some of my cake. Britta and Anna and me usually send letters to each other in a cigar box which slides along a piece of string between their room in North Farmhouse and mine here in Middle Farmhouse.

So I wrote a letter and put it in the cigar box, and then I whistled like we usually whistle when we send each other letters.

In the letter I wrote:

'It just so happens that I have made a sponge cake so I wonder if you would like to come over and try some.'

It took less than two minutes for them to come storming in. They really could not believe that I had made such a lovely sponge cake all by myself. But I said:

'Oh my dears, there is absolutely nothing to it! Anybody could make one.'

We sat in my room and drank squash and ate cake. Immediately afterwards Britta and Anna ran home, because they were going to ask their mum if they could also bake a sponge cake.

It was raining as heavily as before and I didn't know what to do. So I went to Mum again.

'Mum, it's so boring. I really don't know what to do.'

'If I were you I would go and paint the table on the veranda,' said Mum.

Mum seems to believe I can do everything!

She helped me mix the paint in a tin. It was a beautiful green colour. And I got started on the painting. The table began to look very, very nice, just like a new table. While I was painting I wore an old overall so that I wouldn't splash my clothes.

Afterwards I went up to Lasse and Bosse and told them I had painted the veranda table. They jumped out of bed straight away and ran down to look. And then they told Mum that they were completely better and wanted to get dressed immediately so they could start painting as well. Mum let Bosse paint an old tray, and Lasse was allowed to paint a stool. Then Lasse wanted to paint the kitchen bench as well, but Mum said we couldn't turn the whole house green.

All of a sudden Lasse painted a green dot on Bosse's nose. And then, of course, Bosse had to paint one on Lasse's nose. But Lasse ran out of the way. Bosse raced after him with his paint brush held high. Mum arrived just in time to see the paint drip onto the floor. But Bosse was very angry because Lasse didn't have a dot of paint on his nose. So Mum took hold of his brush and painted a dot of green on Lasse's nose, and then she took both brushes away from them.

It's always like that whenever the boys do anything!

Just then Britta and Anna arrived with a sponge cake that they had made. It was as nice as mine, although perhaps mine was a *little* bit spongier.

We all went and sat upstairs in our attic. Bosse climbed through the linden tree to get Olle, so that he could also try Britta and Anna's cake.

It was very nice sitting there in the attic. The rain drummed very hard on the roof above us, and gushed along the gutters. It was lovely to sit there and eat sponge cake and not have to go outside. And it was lovely to be friends again with Britta and Anna.

'Perhaps you didn't tread on the line yesterday evening after all,' said Anna to me.

'I might have trodden on it a tiny bit,' I said.

There are two wooden beams running right across our attic, almost up in the roof. You can climb up there, but it's not easy. That was where the boys stood when they frightened us on New

Year's Eve. Now Lasse suggested we should all climb up there. So we did. It was fun to take a big step from one beam to the other. You could also jump from one beam to the other, but that meant you had to grab hold of the roof very quickly, otherwise you would probably have fallen. As we stood there, Dad came up the attic stairs. We stood in total silence, and Dad didn't see us.

'No, there are no kids up here,' he yelled down to Mum. 'I expect they've climbed through to Olle's.'

And he went downstairs again. Oh, how we laughed! (Later, when we were eating our dinner, we told Dad that we had been standing up under the roof when he came looking for us. And then he said we were proper little rascals.)

When we were standing on the beams Lasse said all at once:

'Look, there's a piece of paper wedged in between the floor beams. Something's written on it.'

We hurried to climb down and read what the paper said. Carefully we went to the attic window where Lasse held out the piece of paper to us. This is what it said:

'Seek the treasure on the isle in the lake. There I have concealed my most precious jewels. Seek in the very midst of the isle.

'One who lived in this place in days gone by.'

'Ooh,' said Anna. 'How exciting! But how strange it sounds.'

'That's how they used to speak in the old days, you know,' said Lasse.

'Just think, precious jewels,' I said. 'Oh, let's try to find where they are! We could get pots of money!'

Britta said nothing.

'We'll go out to the island tomorrow,' said Lasse.

'Yes, let's,' said Bosse and Olle.

Britta still said nothing.

'The isle in the lake.' That could only mean the little island right in the middle of North Farm Lake.

Oh, what fun it was, and very exciting! Rainy days aren't at all boring, really. Anyway, it had stopped raining by now. Britta and Anna and me went off to Grandad's to read the paper to him. Anna and I were so happy when we thought of those jewels that we hopped and skipped, and we wanted to hurry up and tell Grandad. But then Britta said:

'Don't be such idiots! Don't you realize it's one of the boys' usual tricks?'

'Why do you think that?' we asked.

'Well, if that note really had been written by someone who lived at Middle Farmhouse in the old days, surely he wouldn't have written at the bottom: "One who lived in this place in days gone by". It wasn't "days gone by" when he wrote it, was it? Don't you see?'

We hadn't thought of that. But Britta said we should pretend not to know and should go with the boys to the island the next day and look for the jewels.

We Hunt
for Treasure

arly next morning we all set off for the island. We took North Farm's little rowing boat. Lasse rowed. All the time the boys talked about those jewels.

'Know what?' Lasse said to Olle and Bosse. 'I think we'll let the girls have all the jewels, if we find them. Jewels are mostly for girls.'

'Whatever you say,' said Bosse. 'Although we could always sell the jewels and get a load of money for them. But, fine by me—the girls get the jewels.'

'Yep, no problem,' said Olle. 'The girls get the

jewels! Fine by me!'

'Oh, you're so kind,' we said.

'But then you have to find where they are,'
said Lasse, when we had reached the island.
'Bosse and Olle and me will go swimming while
we're waiting.'

'"Seek in the midst of the isle",' said Lasse.
'And shout for us when you find them! Promise!
We want to be there when you find the tin box.'

'How do you know they're in a tin box?' asked
Britta. 'It didn't say that on the note, did it?'

Then Lasse looked a little embarrassed, and he said:

'Well, they have to be in something, I imagine.'

The boys swam and we hunted.

'A tin box? Huh, they'll be sorry,' said Britta.

In the middle of the island was a rocky place, and up on the top of the rocks were a couple of extra stones that hadn't been there before. So it wasn't a particularly difficult hiding place to find. And under those stones there was a rusty tin box. We opened it. Inside was a note, and on the note it said: 'Ha ha, girls will believe anything. One who lived in this place in days gone by.'

Earlier that spring North Farm's ram had been put out to graze on the island. It was full of small, hard pellets he had left behind him. We picked up a few and put them in the tin box. And then we wrote on a new piece of paper which we had brought with us: 'Here are your jewels! Take good care of them because they were dropped by one who lived on this island in days gone by.'

Then we replaced the box under the stones and went to the boys and said it was impossible for us to find the treasure.

'Can't you look while we go swimming?' said Britta.

The boys didn't want to, but eventually they raced off anyway, towards the middle of the island. They were probably going to find an even easier place for us to look. We crept after them, hiding behind the bushes. Exactly like Indians.

The boys had reached the rocky place and Lasse had just taken out the tin box.

'Those girls are useless. They can't even find an easy hiding place like this,' he said.

He shook the box.

'What's that rattling inside?' asked Bosse.

Lasse took off the lid and read the note to Bosse and Olle. Then he hurled the box away from him as far as he could and said:

'There will be revenge for this!'

Then Britta and Anna and me jumped out from behind the bushes and laughed and laughed. We soon told them that we knew from the start that Lasse had made it all up. Then Lasse said that the boys knew that we knew that Lasse had made it up. That was a lie, of course, but to be on the safe side we said we had known that the boys knew that we knew it was only one of Lasse's jokes. And then the boys said—well, I can't be bothered to say it all again, but there was enough 'knew' this and 'knew' that to make your head spin. Then we swam from our flat swimming rocks, and the boys splashed us with lots of water. And we splashed back as much as we could, of course.

Afterwards Lasse thought up the idea that we should make a robbers' den and pretend we were robbers. There is an old hay barn on the island. It isn't used any more, and there's not much left of it, either. The roof is completely broken. Next to the barn is a tall pine tree. We agreed we would have our robbers' den in the barn. Lasse was the robber chief, naturally. He said he was called Robin Hood. Bosse was the second chief and was called Rinaldo Rinaldini. Lasse said we had to rob from the rich to give to the poor, but when we thought about it we didn't know anyone who was rich. And nobody who was poor either, apart from Kristin in Lövnäset.

From time to time Lasse told us we had to go up and keep watch in case any enemy pirate ships were approaching the island. To do that you had to climb along the wall and right across the broken roof and then up into the pine tree. I didn't dare climb all the way to the top of the tree, but Lasse, Bosse and Olle did. Britta and Anna didn't dare climb any higher than me.

But not even the boys saw any enemy pirate ships, even though they kept a look out from the very top.

Lasse told Anna and me to row over to the mainland and find some food to rob. We had to rob from a rich person, he said.

Anna and I rowed off but we couldn't work out who we should rob from. So I went home to Mum and asked if I could rob some food from the larder to take back to the island, since Lasse and Bosse and me didn't plan to be home for dinner. Mum was happy to let me have some. There were cold pancakes with bacon, and sausages and cold potatoes. And I also made masses of cheese sandwiches. I put it all in a basket. Mum came and gave me ten freshly-baked cinnamon buns as well, and a big bottle of milk.

Then I ran to Anna's house. She had a basket full of food too. She had meatballs and cold roast pork and a whole loaf and fruit soup in a flask and six slices of cold rice pudding.

When we got back to the robbers' den, Lasse looked very satisfied.

'Good,' he said. 'Did you put your own life at risk robbing that?'

Anna and I didn't really know how to answer that, but we said we had only put our own lives at risk a tiny bit.

'Good,' said Lasse again.

We laid everything out on a flat rock outside our robbers' den, and we lay on our stomachs and ate. As we were tucking in Bosse said:

'Listen, Robin Hood, you said we had to give to a poor person. You mustn't lie there and gobble up all the food yourself!'

'I am a poor person,' said Lasse, helping himself to another pancake.

We passed round the milk and the fruit soup and we each took a mouthful when we were thirsty. Finally we had eaten up everything except two cheese sandwiches, which we hid in the robbers' den.

Oh, we had such a lot of fun all day on that island! We swam masses of times, and climbed trees, and for a while we split into two separate bands of robbers. Britta and Anna and me were one band, and we lived in the robbers' den and had to defend it from the boys' band. We had sticks which we pretended were rifles. Britta stood on guard in the doorway, Anna looked out through the window, and I peered out through the broken roof. But I got tired of doing that because it was so difficult trying to stay up there.

So I climbed down and stood beside Anna. And guess what? That's exactly when the boys climbed up the back wall of the barn where we couldn't see them.

All of a sudden they came jumping down through the broken roof and took us prisoner and said we would be shot. Just when we were about to be shot, Lasse yelled:

'Enemy ship in sight!'

It was Oskar, our farmhand, rowing across the lake to fetch us. He said it was nine o'clock and he asked us what kind of daft chumps we were who didn't have the sense to go home when it was night-time. Do you know, we had no idea that it was so late!

'Don't you lot never get hungry?' said Oskar crossly.

And at that moment I noticed that I did feel a bit hungry.

Mum and Dad had eaten dinner ages ago. But there were sandwiches and milk and hard boiled eggs on the kitchen table for us when we got home.

Anna and I
Make People Happy

When we went back to school last autumn, our teacher told us one day that we should always try to make people happy. We should never do things that make people sad, our teacher said. Later that afternoon Anna and I were sitting on our kitchen steps and chatting, and we agreed that we would start making people happy right away. But the worst thing was, we weren't sure how to go about it. We decided to begin with Agda, who helps Mum in the house. We went in to the kitchen to see her. She was on her knees, scrubbing the floor.

'Don't step on the floor while it's wet,' she said.

'Agda,' I said. 'Can you tell us something we can do to make you happy?'

'Yes. If you would get out of the kitchen while I'm scrubbing the floor I would be tremendously happy,' said Agda.

We went back out. *That* wasn't a particularly nice way to make people happy. And I don't expect that's what our teacher meant, either.

Mum was busy in the garden, picking apples. I went to her and said:

'Mum, tell me something I can do to make you happy.'

'I'm already happy,' said Mum.

That was so annoying! But I didn't want to give up, so I said:

'But perhaps I could do something to make you even happier?'

'You don't have to do anything except carry on being my good little girl,' said Mum. 'That will make me more than happy.'

Then I went back to Anna and told her that

our teacher had no idea how hard it was to find someone you could make happy.

'Let's try Grandad,' said Anna.

So we went to Grandad.

'Is that my little friends coming to say hello?' said Grandad. 'That has made me very happy!'

Well, that was just as annoying! We had only walked through the door and Grandad was happy already! If this carried on there would be nothing for us to do.

'No, Grandad,' said Anna. 'Don't tell us that you are already happy. We want to do something to *make* you happy. You'll have to help us think of something, because our teacher has said that we've got to make other people happy.'

'You could read the paper for me, perhaps,' said Grandad.

We supposed we could do that, of course, but we did that so often there was nothing special about it.

Then suddenly Anna said:

'Poor you, Grandad, sitting up here in your room all the time. Wouldn't it make you very happy if we took you for a walk?'

Grandad didn't look particularly keen on that idea, but he promised to come with us for a walk.

So off we went. Anna and I walked one on each side of Grandad, guiding him, because of course Grandad can't see where he is going. We took him all around Noisy Village and chatted and told him things the whole time. It began to get windy and it started to rain a little, but we didn't care because all we thought about was making Grandad happy.

As we were walking along Grandad said:

'Do you think this is long enough now? I would like to go and have a lie down.'

So we led Grandad back to his room and he immediately undressed and got into his bed, even though it wasn't evening yet. Anna tucked him in. Grandad did look rather tired. Before we left, Anna said:

'Grandad, what is the nicest thing that has happened to you today?'

We thought, both of us, that he would say the walk had been the nicest thing. But Grandad said:

'The nicest thing today? Well, that was when I could climb into my comfy bed, because I feel so tired and peculiar.'

Then Anna and I had to do our homework, so we had no time to make anyone else happy that day. We weren't really sure, either, if we were making people happy in the right way. That's why we decided to ask our teacher the next day what you should actually do. Our teacher said that often you don't need to do much at all. You could perhaps sing a song for someone who was ill and alone, or give a flower to someone who never usually gets flowers, or be friendly to someone who felt shy and out of place.

Anna and I decided to try again, and that afternoon I heard Agda telling Mum that Kristin in Lövnäset was ill. I ran to Anna straight away and said:

'We're in luck! Kristin in Lövnäset is ill. Come on, let's go there and sing!'

I think Kristin was quite glad to see us, but she might have been wondering why we hadn't brought anything in a basket for her. We usually do. But we thought she would be really happy once we started singing.

'Shall we sing something for you, Kristin?' I

said.

'Sing,' said Kristin, looking astonished. 'Why?'

'To make you happy,' said Anna.

'Oh, well, all right. Sing if you like,' said Kristin.

And so we burst out singing 'Borgmäster Munte' so it echoed around the cottage. And then we sang 'Cold Blows the Northern Wind', all seven verses. I couldn't quite see that Kristin looked any happier than when we started. That's why we chose 'Farewell My Father' and 'Sleep, Little Pussy Willow' and 'In the Humble Fishing Hut' and a few other tunes, but they didn't make Kristin any happier. Anna and I were almost starting to get hoarse, but we didn't want to stop until we had made Kristin really happy, even if it was hard work. We were just about to get started on 'Up There No Death Shall Be' when Kristin pulled herself out of her bed and said:

'Sing, you two, as much as you like! I'm going out for a while.'

But Anna and I thought it wasn't worth

trying any longer, so we said goodbye to Kristin.

'Perhaps it will work better if we give flowers to someone who never usually gets flowers,' said Anna.

We were walking along, wondering who we could find to give flowers to, when we saw our farmhand, Oskar, go into the barn. We ran to catch up with him and I said:

'Oskar, have you ever been given any flowers?'

'Oh no, I'm not dead n' gone yet,' said Oskar.

Poor thing, I'm sure he thought you only got flowers at your funeral. Anna looked at me and her face lit up because we had found somebody so quickly who never got any flowers. We ran straight off to North Farm's meadow and picked a bunch of heather. It was a really beautiful bunch, and we took it with us back to the barn. There was Oskar with his wheelbarrow, taking manure to the manure heap which is right behind the barn.

'Here you are, Oskar, some flowers for you,' we said, and held out the bunch of heather.

Oskar thought we were making fun of him at first, and he didn't want to take the flowers, but we said he *had* to take them, so he did. A short while afterwards, when Anna and I were looking for a rabbit that had escaped, we happened to walk past the manure heap. There on top of the manure heap lay Oskar's bunch of flowers.

'I'm starting to believe our teacher has got it wrong,' said Anna.

We decided to stop trying to make people happy, but later in the afternoon, when Anna and I walked into our kitchen, there was a man sitting on one of the chairs, looking stupid. Svensson from Stubbnäset was his name. He was here to buy a pig from us, and Lasse and Bosse had run to fetch Dad who was ploughing over in the big field. Svensson was sitting in our kitchen, waiting. Anna dragged me to a corner and whispered:

'Don't you think he looks shy and out of place? What if we had one more go, after all? Talk to him and try to cheer him up, you know, like our teacher said.'

So that's what we decided to do. Usually Anna and I can talk non-stop, but now, when we were supposed to be talking to make Svensson happy, it was totally impossible to think of anything to say. I thought and thought, and at last I said:

'Lovely weather today.'

Svensson didn't answer, so I tried again.

'Lovely weather today,' I said.

'Yup,' said Svensson.

Then it went completely quiet. After a moment I said:

'It was lovely weather yesterday too.'

'Yup,' said Svensson.

I looked at Anna, because I thought she ought to be helping me. So then Anna said:

'Looks like it's going to be lovely weather tomorrow, as well.'

'Yup,' said Svensson.

Just then Dad came into the farmyard and Svensson stood up and went. But just after he had gone out through the door, he stuck his head back in, grinned, and said:

'What was the weather like the day before yesterday?'

'Perhaps we made him a *little* bit happy, at least,' Anna said afterwards.

'Possibly,' I said. 'But that's enough now. I'm

not thinking of making another single person happy.'

But in fact I did. And so did Anna. Because the next day our teacher told us that a girl in our class, called Märta, would be away from school for a long time. She had a serious illness and would have to stay in bed for many months. That evening, before I fell asleep, I lay there thinking about Märta, and that's when I decided to give her Bella, my best doll. I knew Märta had no toys at all.

In the morning I told Anna that I was going to give my doll to Märta, so Anna went and fetched her best storybook. When school was over we ran to Märta's house. She was lying in her bed, looking very pale. Never have I seen anyone look as happy as Märta did when we put Bella and the storybook on her blanket and said she could keep them both. Oh my, how happy she was! She hugged Bella and the storybook and all she did was laugh. Then she shouted to her mum to come and look.

When we were outside again I said to Anna: 'Oh, now we've made someone happy without

even thinking about it.'

Anna was very surprised. She said:

'It was probably good that we didn't start singing to Märta, because as far as I'm concerned people are happier when they get dolls and books.'

'Yes. Children, at least,' I said.

Grandad's
Eightieth Birthday

Last Sunday it was Grandad's eightieth birthday. We got up early here in Noisy Village, I can tell you, and at eight o'clock we went to Grandad's, all of us. There was Dad and Mum and Lasse and Bosse and me and Agda and Oskar from here at Middle Farm, Uncle Nils and Auntie Lisa and Olle, and even little Kerstin, from South Farm, and everyone from North Farm of course. Auntie Greta, Britta and Anna's mum, had prepared a beautiful breakfast tray. And we all had flowers with us for Grandad.

Grandad was already up and dressed and

sitting in his rocking chair, looking so smart and gentle. All of us children sang to him, and Uncle Erik gave a speech. This is what he said at the end of his speech:

'No one has ever had a father like mine!'

Then Grandad cried, and the tears dropped down onto his beard. I very nearly started crying too.

All day letters and telegrams and flowers arrived for Grandad.

'Heh, heh, heh, to think that folks remember an old codger like me,' said Grandad.

We stayed with Grandad, all of us children, because it was such fun to read out his letters and telegrams.

I wonder exactly how many times Grandad said 'Heh, heh, heh' on his birthday. Mainly he sat there ever so silently in his rocking chair, but now and then he said:

'Eighty years. Imagine being that old, heh, heh, heh.'

After he had said it for the fifth time Anna ran up and took hold of Grandad's arm and said:

'Grandad, promise that you won't ever die!'

But Grandad didn't answer. Instead he patted Anna on the cheek and said:

'Dear child, dear child.'

When the letters and telegrams had stopped arriving we read the newspaper for Grandad. And do you know what? In one place in the newspaper it said:

'Former landowner and farmer Anders Johan Andersson of North Farm, Noisy Village, is 80 years old on Sunday the 18th October.'

We read that out to Grandad and he nodded and looked very contented, and said:

'Well, well, I'm even in the newspaper, heh, heh, heh!'

I couldn't understand that 'former landowner and farmer Anders Johan Andersson' meant Grandad. It could just as easily have said:

'Grandad in Noisy Village is 80 on Sunday.'

We read the whole newspaper to Grandad, but every so often he wanted us to read that bit about 'former landowner and farmer' again. Anyway, the paper was only filled with bad news, all about how it might be war, war, and more war.

'Think if the war comes here and destroys all

of Noisy Village,' said Bosse. 'Do you think it will, Grandad?'

'Oh no, I don't think it will. I'm sure God will hold his hand over little Noisy Village.'

'I really hope so, because I want to live in Noisy Village as long as I live' said Britta.

Britta and Anna and I have come up with a good idea. We think Lasse can marry Britta when he grows up, and they can live in Middle Farmhouse, and Bosse can marry Anna and live in North Farmhouse, and Olle can marry me and live in South Farmhouse. In that way we can stay here in Noisy Village, all of us. As we were sitting there in Grandad's room, we told the boys our plan. But then Lasse said:

'Ha! I think I want a more beautiful wife than Britta!'

And Bosse said that when he grew up he would travel to America and be an Indian chief and marry an Indian girl called Laughing Water or something like that.

'That'll sound good when you're shouting to her!' said Lasse. 'Laughing Water, is the coffee ready? Laughing Water, have you put the potatoes on?'

But Bosse said of course they wouldn't be eating potatoes, because Bosse didn't like potatoes.

Olle said he wanted to live in South Farmhouse with Kerstin when he grew up.

'But if I really must get married, then I might as well take Lisa. But I'm not making any promises!'

Oh, such stupid boys! But they'll soon see. We'll marry them whether they want us to or not. We ought to be allowed to decide something for once! Well, I'm planning to marry Olle, at least. It's just a pity he has so little hair. But perhaps it will get longer by the time he's grown.

Grandad laughed as he heard what we were talking about. And he said:

'Heh, heh, heh, it's a long time to go until then. And it's good to be children as long as you can.'

When Grandad grew tired we said goodnight to him and went home. It was pitch black outside, and Lasse and Bosse and I went with Olle to his kitchen door, so that he wouldn't have to walk on his own in the dark.

Well, there really is nothing more I can tell you about us Noisy Village children. I've got to go to bed because tomorrow we are all going out to collect the potatoes. We have been given three days off from school to get it done.

It's so much fun collecting the potatoes. We wear our oldest clothes and have wellington boots on our feet. Sometimes it's rather cold out in the potato field, and our fingers go all stiff. But we blow on them.

A little while ago I got a letter in the cigar box from Britta and Anna.

This is what the letter said:

'Guess what, Lisa? We've thought up a good plan. Wait until we get out into the potato field and we can play a really good trick on the boys. Ha ha, it will be so funny. They will get very angry.'

I wonder what exactly their plan could be. But I'll find out tomorrow.

Noisy Village is only a small place. There are just three farmhouses, and only six children. But there's plenty of fun and adventures to be had. Join the children of Noisy Village as they play at being shipwrecked pirates, bring a little lamb to school, and camp out under the stars by a lake.

I get a Lamb

Spring is probably the best time of all. Anna and I always try to work out when it's most fun. Anna thinks it's most fun in the summer and I think it's most fun in the spring. And at Christmas too, of course. Anna thinks that as well.

Now I'm going to tell you about something that happened last spring. We've got masses of sheep here in Noisy Village and they have lambs every spring. Lambs are the sweetest things ever. They are sweeter than kittens and puppies and piglets. I almost think they are sweeter than Kerstin, but I daren't say that in case Olle hears.

When the sheep are lambing we usually run

down to the sheep shed every morning to see how many lambs have arrived during the night. When you open the door of the sheep shed all the sheep bleat their heads off. The lambs sound so lovely and cute when they bleat, not croaky like the ewes and the rams. Almost every ewe has two lambs.

One Sunday morning when I went down to the sheep shed I caught sight of a lamb lying dead in the straw. I ran to Dad straight away and told him, and he went to find out why the lamb had died. It was because its mother didn't have any milk in her udder. That poor, poor lamb, he had died because he didn't get any food! I sat in the doorway of the sheep shed and cried. After a while Anna came and heard all about it, and she cried as well.

'I don't want lambs to die,' I said to Dad.

'No, no one wants that,' said Dad. 'But sadly enough here is another one that has to die.'

He showed me the tiny lamb that he was holding in his arms, and it looked so pitiful. It was the dead lamb's brother. Of course he couldn't get any milk from his mummy either, and milk is the only thing a new born lamb can have. That's why Dad said we had to kill the dead lamb's brother so that he wouldn't have to starve to death. When we heard that, Anna and I cried even more. We cried an awful lot.

'I don't want lambs to die!' I howled, and threw myself on the floor.

Then Dad lifted me up and said: 'Don't cry, Lisa!' And then he said:

'I'll let you try feeding this lamb with a bottle, if you like. Just like a newborn baby.'

Oh, that made me so happy, happier than I think I have ever been before! I didn't know you could feed lambs like you do newborn babies. Dad said I shouldn't be too hopeful. He thought the lamb would probably die in any case, but we could always try.

Anna and I ran to Auntie Lisa, Olle's mum, and she let us borrow a bottle and a teat that Kerstin had drunk her milk from when she was really tiny. Then we ran back to Dad again.

'Dad, can't we give him some cream, the poor little thing?' I asked.

But Dad said that if I gave the lamb cream he

would get ill. His tummy could only cope with milk that had been diluted with water. Dad helped me mix the milk and then we warmed the bottle in hot water. Then I pushed the teat into the lamb's mouth. And do you know what? He started sucking straight away. You could see he was hungry all right.

'So, now you are this lamb's foster mother,' Dad said. 'But he has to have food from the crack of dawn to late at night, so you mustn't get bored with doing it.'

Anna said that if I got bored with doing it I only had to tell her because she would love to feed the lamb for me. But I said:

'Ha! You needn't think anyone gets bored feeding lambs!'

I called the lamb Pontus, and Dad said it would be my very own lamb. It was lucky it was all decided before Lasse and Bosse woke up, otherwise there would have been a quarrel over Pontus, I'm sure of that.

Noisy Village is a small place. There are just three farmhouses and only six children, but there's plenty of fun and adventures to be had. Join the children of Noisy Village as they rescue a lonely dog, search for a secret treasure map, and get caught in a snow storm!

ABOUT THE AUTHOR

Astrid Lindgren was born in 1907, and grew up at a farm called Näs in the south of Sweden. Her first book was published in 1944, followed a year later by *Pippi Longstocking*. She wrote 34 chapter books and 41 picture books, that all together have sold 165 million copies worldwide. Her books have been translated into 107 different languages and according to UNESCO's annual list, she is the 18th most translated author in the world.

She created stories about Pippi, a free-spirited, red-haired girl to entertain her daughter, Karin, who was ill with pneumonia. The girl's name 'Pippi Longstocking' was in fact invented by Karin. Astrid Lindgren once commented about her work, 'I write to amuse the child within me, and can only hope that other children may have some fun that way, too.'

For more information visit **www.astridlindgren.com**